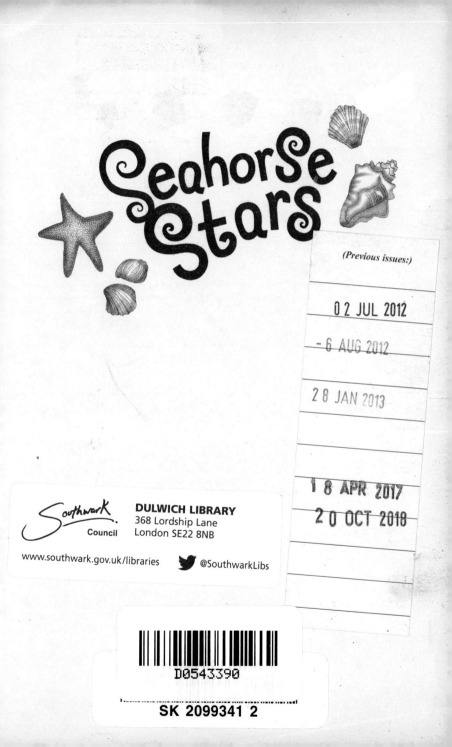

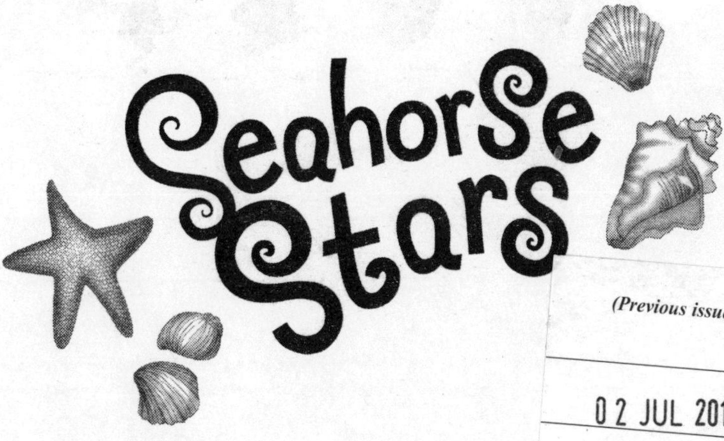
Seahorse Stars

Seahorse Stars

Danger in the Deep

Zuzu Singer

Illustrated by Helen Turner

USBORNE

Meet the Pearlies

Fun and friendly CAMMIE is a vivid pink seahorse who dreams of becoming a Seahorse Star.

Shy but sweet CORA is a pretty pink seahorse with pale pink stripes.

Bossyboots CORINETTA is a golden seahorse with a snooty upturned nose.

Cammie's best friend JESS is a born storyteller. She is a bright bluey-green.

# of Rainbow Reef

Pale-green
MISS SWISH
is firm but fair
as the elegant
leader of
the Pearlies.

Brainbox BREE
knows all the answers!
She is purple with lovely
lavender fins.

Fast and fearless
FIZZ has bold red and
yellow stripes and is
ready for anything!

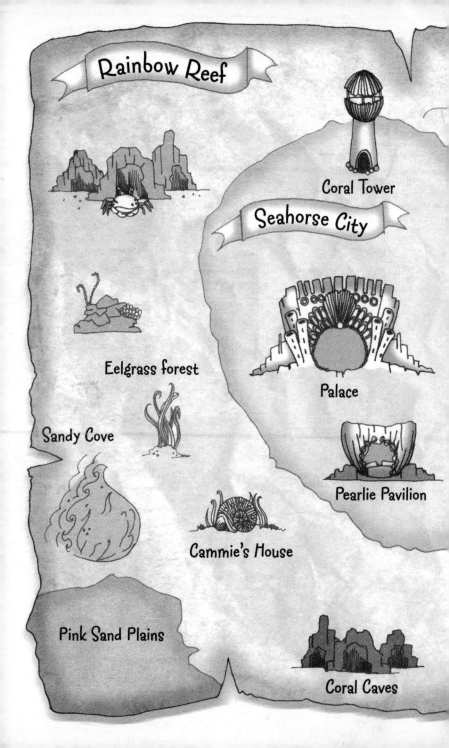

Seahorse Stars is dedicated to every child who
loves to read...including you!

First published in the UK in 2011 by Usborne Publishing Ltd., Usborne
House, 83-85 Saffron Hill, London EC1N 8RT, England.
www.usborne.com

Text copyright © Lee Weatherly, 2011

Illustration copyright © Usborne Publishing Ltd., 2011

The right of Lee Weatherly to be identified as the author of this work
has been asserted by her in accordance with the Copyright, Designs and
Patents Act, 1988.

The name Usborne and the devices ♀⊕ are Trade Marks of
Usborne Publishing Ltd.

A CIP catalogue record for this book is available from the British Library.

JFMA JJASOND/11 02342/1

ISBN 9781409520276 Printed in Reading, Berkshire, UK.

Chapter One

Cammie Sunbeam smiled as she and her best friend Jess swam up to the Pearlie Pavilion. It was almost time for another Pearlie meeting. She could hardly wait!

The other Pearlies were waiting outside for the doors to open. Joining them, Cammie could see seahorses of every colour of the rainbow, and more besides. She herself was a bright, cheerful pink, and Jess a pretty blue-green.

"I wonder what our next pearl will be for?" said Cammie eagerly. She gazed up at the three shiny pearls that sat on her crown. She'd won them for her camping, first-aid and map-reading skills, and she was very proud of them.

Jess spun in place in the warm water. "Miss Swish said we'd find out today," she said. "Just think, only three more pearls and we'll be Seahorse Stars!"

Cammie's fins tingled at the thought. The Seahorse Stars were the waviest club in Rainbow Reef. They got to go on exciting adventures, and do things to help the Reef. She could hardly wait to be one!

"*I* know what our next pearl is for," said a seahorse called Fizz, swimming over to them. "I heard Miss Swish talking with one of the other leaders." Fizz had red and yellow stripes, and was very sporty. She was in the Dancing Waves group along with Cammie and Jess.

"Oh, what?" cried Cammie and Jess together. They bobbed up and down in the water.

But Fizz just smiled. "I'm not saying. It should be a lot of fun, though!"

Two more seahorses came swimming over: Bree and Cora, who were also in the Dancing Waves. "Are you talking about our next pearl?" asked Bree, fluttering her purple fins. Bree was the cleverest seahorse in their group, but so nice that the others didn't mind!

"Yes, Fizz knows what it is, but she won't tell us," groaned Jess.

A stuck-up golden seahorse called Corinetta had overheard. She was in the Dancing Waves too — unfortunately for them, thought Cammie!

"Oh, I'll bet you don't know at all," she sneered at Fizz.

Fizz frowned. "I do too!"

"Ha! Prove it, then!" said Corinetta.

"All right, I will," said Fizz angrily. "Our next pearl is going to be for Sea Safety — so there!"

Cora gave a nervous squeal. "*Sea Safety?*" she gasped. "But...but I've heard that's really dangerous!" Cora was pale pink, and scared of everything!

"No, it isn't," Bree assured Cora. "We learn

how to be safe — that's the opposite of dangerous."

Corinetta scowled. "You're just making that up," she said to Fizz. "You don't know what our next pearl is, any more than we do!"

Fizz started to say something, but before she could, the doors to the Pearlie Pavilion swung open. "Hello, girls!" called one of the group leaders. "Come in, and let's get started."

Cammie felt tingly with excitement as she swam inside with the others. She hoped Fizz was right. Sea Safety sounded amazing!

The Pearlie Pavilion was a round building made of pink coral, with different cosy areas for all the groups. Up above, the ceiling was open, so that you could see families of fish and even sea turtles swimming past.

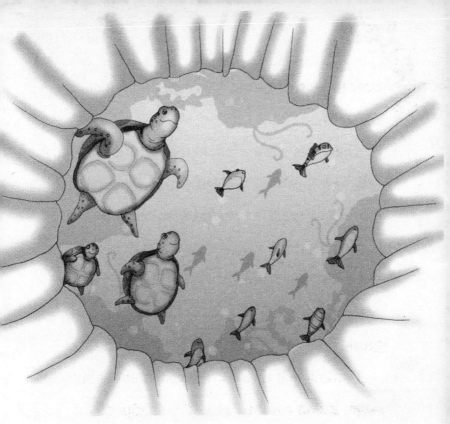

The girls headed over to the Dancing Waves

area. Fizz and Corinetta were still glaring at

each other. "Just wait, you'll see," said Fizz.

Corinetta sniffed. "I'll bet!"

Jess rolled her eyes. "Oh, stop it, you two,"

she said as they settled down in pink and white

chairs made of shells. "We'll *all* find out soon enough!"

"Find out what?" asked their group leader Miss Swish, who'd just arrived. She was a tall, pale-green seahorse. Miss Swish could be firm at times, but she was very kind and understanding, thought Cammie. And she knew everything there was about becoming a Seahorse Star!

"Nothing, Miss Swish," said Fizz sheepishly.

Miss Swish looked as if she didn't believe her, but she smiled. "All right, shall we get started? I'm sure you all want to find out about your next pearl!"

"We certainly do," muttered Corinetta, narrowing her eyes at Fizz.

At the front of the area was a piece of slate on a coral stand. Miss Swish wrote on it with a piece of chalk held in her tail. "Your next pearl will be for...Sea Safety!" She wrote the words in big letters, underlining them.

Sea Safety

Sea Safety! Fizz had been right! Cammie bounced in her seat. The others all looked pleased as well. Especially Fizz, who shot a triumphant look at Corinetta.

"See!" she hissed.

Corinetta scowled. "Lucky guess," she grumbled.

Cora raised a fin. "Miss Swish, it's not dangerous, is it?" she squeaked timidly.

"No, but it *is* serious," said Miss Swish. "It's very important that you learn how to be safe, both here in Rainbow Reef and out in the Deep."

The Deep! The Dancing Waves fell silent. Cammie swallowed hard. The Deep was the sea that lay beyond warm, friendly Rainbow Reef. She'd heard it was dark and cold, and full of strange, frightening creatures.

19

Cora's lower lip trembled. "We...we won't have to go *into* the Deep, will we?" she quavered.

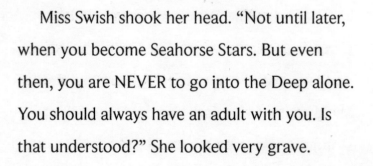

Miss Swish shook her head. "Not until later, when you become Seahorse Stars. But even then, you are NEVER to go into the Deep alone. You should always have an adult with you. Is that understood?" She looked very grave.

The girls all nodded hard. Cammie felt relieved. Though she was curious about the Deep, she was happy to wait until she was a Seahorse Star to actually go there!

"What will we have to do to earn our pearl?" asked Jess eagerly.

This was the question they all wanted to know the answer to. Cammie leaned forward with the others.

"Over the next few weeks, I'm going to tell you about the different creatures in Rainbow Reef and the Deep," explained Miss Swish. "You'll find out which ones are safe, which ones to avoid, and which places you should *never* go." She wrote *KEEP OUT!* on the board in big letters.

"To earn your pearl, you'll need to show me

that you've learned these things," she went on. "You can make a poster, or write a story, or even do a dance — it's up to you. But whatever you do, you'll need to show that you've learned all about Sea Safety."

Cammie and Jess exchanged an excited glance. Fizz was right, thought Cammie. Sea Safety was going to be a lot of fun!

"Does everyone understand?" Miss Swish looked around and smiled. "Good! Then let's get started."

Chapter Two

The girls watched as Miss Swish drew a map of Rainbow Reef. "Now then, here in Rainbow Reef, we're very safe," she began. "The creatures are all friendly, and there are few dangers...thanks to our guards!"

She smiled at Cammie, who beamed back. Cammie was very proud of her mother, who was one of the guards who kept Rainbow Reef safe.

"Even so, you should still know as much about the Reef as you can," said Miss Swish. "Let's start with who lives here!" Pointing to her map with a piece of reed, she told them where each type of creature in the Reef lived — the seahorses, the crabs, the sea turtles, and all the different kinds of fish.

Cammie listened carefully. She was determined to learn all about Sea Safety, so that she could do a really good project. More than that, she knew that Miss Swish was right. This was an important pearl to earn if they wanted to be Seahorse Stars!

"There are also some places in Rainbow Reef that you should avoid," went on Miss

Swish. "For instance, there's a wobbly section of coral here —" she pointed with her fin — "and a whirlpool here. Both of these places have signs saying *Danger*, so if you see one of these signs, stay well away!"

Fizz blinked. "What's so dangerous about a whirlpool? All it does is spin you around in a circle."

"Yes, but this is quite a large one," explained Miss Swish. "Small creatures like seahorses could be badly injured if they were caught in it for long."

Bree raised her fin. "What should we do if we get caught in the whirlpool by mistake?"

Cora gave a whimper. "Don't worry," whispered Cammie. "It would never happen!"

Miss Swish overheard. "Well, I hope not. But do you all remember the storm a few months ago, that swept us away from our first camping trip? What if one of you had landed in the whirlpool as a result?"

Cammie's fins grew cold. What a scary thought!

"So you see, it's important to know these things," Miss Swish went on. "If you get caught in the whirlpool by mistake, don't try to fight it, or you'll just grow weak. Eventually, the whirlpool's current will return you to the edge of the pool. When that happens, swim as hard as you can and dart free! All right?"

Everyone nodded hard. Cammie felt dizzy just imagining being in the whirlpool. She hoped it never happened!

Miss Swish told them a few more things about Rainbow Reef, and then she wiped her slate clean.

"Now then," she said seriously. "It's time to talk about the Deep."

That night Cammie's mind was buzzing with all she'd learned. She could hardly wait to tell her family about it!

"Mum, Dad, did you know that we seahorses have a cousin called the sea dragon?" she asked. They were sitting at their coral table, with bowls of Dad's delicious plankton stew in front of them.

Mum smiled. "Yes, but tell us about it anyway," she said. "Tigg and Stripe might like to hear."

Stripe, her little brother, had wide eyes. "Do we *really*?" he asked. He and Cammie's little sister Tigg were twins, and looked almost exactly alike — right down to the stripes on their orange and black tails!

Cammie nodded, taking a slurp of stew. "Yes, he lives in the Deep. Only he likes to be left alone. So Miss Swish said if we ever see him

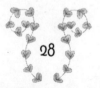

we should pretend we haven't, and he'll be grateful."

Cammie paused, thinking of the sea dragon. She thought he sounded very interesting. What a shame that he liked to keep to himself. She'd love to meet him, and see what the seahorses' cousin looked like.

"How stuck up," muttered Tigg. "He probably thinks he's too good to be around other people. Like some *brothers* I could mention!" She gave Stripe an angry look. He flushed and didn't answer.

Cammie stared at her little sister in surprise. Were she and Stripe having a row?

Mum caught Cammie's gaze and shook her head, as if warning Cammie not to ask. "It sounds like Miss Swish is teaching you really

well," she said aloud. "What else did you learn today?"

"Yes, tell us all about it," said Dad with a smile. "Tigg, sit up straight," he added. "You'll get a cramp in your tail, slouching like that!"

Looking sulky, Tigg sat up a little, still scowling at Stripe. He ignored her.

Cammie thought. "Well, there's the snapping sea turtle," she said. "You have to be really careful around him, because he might snap at you. And there are giant squids, and do you know what *they* might do?"

"What?" cried Stripe, bouncing in the water.

"Shoot black goo at you!" exclaimed Cammie. "And then, when you can't see, they eat you right up."

"They don't, not really!" screeched Stripe
in delight.

"Yes they do, don't they, Mum?" said
Cammie.

Their mother nodded with a smile. "Yes, but
they're not very clever. If you see one coming,
you can often get away from it, if you keep
your wits about you."

"And there are sharks, too," went on Cammie excitedly. "They don't even shoot black goo at you, they just gulp you right down – snip, snap!" She bit at the air, pretending to be a shark.

Tigg was still frowning. "Well, I hope a shark comes along and eats *you*," she muttered to her brother. "Mum, Dad, I've had enough. May I be excused?" Without waiting for an answer, she swam off towards the bedroom she shared with Cammie.

Stripe glared after her. "As if I care what *you* think," he called. But he looked cross, and a moment later he asked to be excused, too.

Cammie was trying not to laugh. "What's up with them?" she asked once Stripe had swum off to his room. She helped herself to more stew.

Dad sighed. "Stripe has a new friend — a boy whose family has just moved into the next coral cave," he explained. "The two of them were playing on their own today. I think Tigg got her tail a bit out of joint."

"Oh," said Cammie. Poor Tigg! She and Stripe were very close. It must have been awful for her not to have her twin to play with, even for an afternoon.

When Cammie said this out loud, her mother nodded. "Yes, I'm sure it wasn't easy for her. It's good practice, though. She and Stripe will be going to Seahorse School soon, and they won't always be in the same class. They need to learn to do without each other sometimes."

"Don't worry, they'll sort it out between them," added Dad. He grinned, and nudged Cammie with his tail. "Come on, help us do the dishes. You can tell us what you need to do to get your pearl!"

By the time she went to bed that night, Tigg was already asleep and Cammie had forgotten all about her little sister's problem. All she could think of was Sea Safety, and earning her next pearl.

What shall I do for my project? she wondered as she lay snuggled in her seaweed bed. It had to be something really special, but what? Then her gaze fell on the pretty shells that made a pattern on her wall. She gasped. Of course!

Cammie fell asleep smiling. She knew

exactly what she was going to do...and it was

going to be the waviest project of all!

Chapter Three

For the next few Pearlie meetings, Miss Swish
continued to teach the Dancing Waves about
Sea Safety. Finally the time came for them
to start working on their projects. Jess
came home from school with Cammie one
afternoon, so that they could work on
them together.

"I'm going to write a story," said Jess, dropping her school books on Cammie's sandy bedroom floor. "What are you going to do?"

Cammie hadn't told anyone her idea yet. She smiled proudly. "I'm going to make a mosaic," she said.

Jess stared at her. "A *what*?"

"A mosaic," repeated Cammie, her eyes shining. "It's a poster, but instead of drawing on it, I'll make pictures with shells and pebbles and things. I got the idea from those shells on the wall." She pointed with her fin.

"Wavy!" exclaimed Jess. "No one else will be doing that. Great idea, Cammie!"

The two girls started to work. Cammie had already gathered her supplies, choosing the prettiest pebbles and small shells she could find.

She also had a large piece of eelgrass to paste them onto, and a pot of crab glue.

"My mosaic's going to be a map," she said. "It'll show where all the dangers are in Rainbow Reef and the Deep."

Jess had started to write. "My story's about a seahorse called *Jessy*," she said with a grin. "She's very naughty and does all the things you shouldn't. And then she wishes she had listened!"

Cammie giggled. The story sounded just right for Jess. She could hardly wait to read it!

Tigg came swimming into the room. "Hi," she said glumly. "What are you doing?"

"Our projects for Pearlies," said Cammie. "Do you want to see?" She couldn't help feeling sorry for her little sister. Stripe still hadn't tired of his new friend, and Tigg had been moping about the house for weeks now.

Tigg swam over. "What's it going to be?" she asked, looking at the shells and pebbles.

Cammie explained, and described what she had planned for each part of the mosaic. "And I'm going to have the sea dragon here!" she finished up. She pointed to where the edge of the Deep would be.

Tigg wrinkled her nose. "Oh, the sea dragon," she said. "He's the one who's so stuck up."

Jess looked up from her story. "No, he's not," she said. Her eyes were sparkling with mischief. "Why, Tigg, didn't you know that the sea dragon is magical?"

Tigg's jaw dropped open. So did Cammie's!

"He *is*?" gasped Tigg.

"Oh, yes," said Jess. "Why, he's one of the most magical creatures in the whole sea! That's why he likes to be on his own. It helps his magic powers grow stronger."

Cammie started to say something, and then stopped. For the first time in weeks, Tigg had lost her gloomy look. Perhaps it wouldn't hurt for Jess to spin her a wild story.

"What sort of magic does he have?" asked Tigg, swimming close to Jess.

"Oh, all sorts," said Jess seriously. "He's a very powerful magician, you know. He can change colour, and he can cast spells, and he can even…" She lowered her voice. "He can even grant wishes!"

"He *can*?" Tigg's eyes grew wide.

Jess nodded. "Yes, all the creatures go to him when they want a wish granted. He gets very tired of it. That's why he wants to be left alone."

Cammie was struggling to hold back her laughter. "I thought you said he wanted to be alone to make his magic grow stronger," she pointed out.

"That, too," said Jess. She gave a cough

that sounded a lot like a giggle.

Tigg was staring at her. "Jess, is this all true?" she asked. "I mean, really, *really* true?"

"Of course!" said Jess cheerfully. "And that's not even half of it. Why—"

Cammie decided this had gone far enough. "No, it's not true," she broke in. "Jess is only teasing you, Tigg. Now come on, leave us alone so we can work."

"No!" cried Tigg, bobbing in the water. "I want to hear more about the sea dragon!"

"*Tigg*," groaned Cammie. She shooed her towards the door. "Go on, now. Go play or something."

"I can't, I don't have anyone to play with!" burst out Tigg. "I want to stay here with you and Jess, and hear more about the sea dragon.

Can't I, please? Please?" She folded her fins under her chin, pleading.

"There's nothing to hear," insisted Cammie. "He's just a cousin to the seahorses, that's all. There's nothing magical about him."

"But Jess said there is!" cried Tigg, churning the water with her tail. "She said that all the creatures go to him, and—"

"I was just teasing, Tigg," said Jess. "It's not *really* true."

"It's...not?" whispered Tigg. She seemed so crestfallen that Cammie almost laughed, but she knew it would be mean.

Then her little sister's chin jerked up. "I don't believe you!" she said loudly. "You're just saying that to make me go away. Well, fine, I will!" And she shot off in a trail of bubbles.

"Jess, why did you *tell* her all that?" groaned Cammie. "She's in a proper state now."

Jess looked embarrassed. "I was just trying it out for my story," she said. "That's what Jessy thinks, and it gets her in a lot of trouble. Should I go after Tigg and explain?"

Cammie shook her head. There was no

reasoning with Tigg when she got so cross. "No, don't worry about it. She'll forget about it soon." Then despite herself, Cammie started to giggle. The expression on Tigg's face when Jess told her about the sea dragon really *had* been funny!

Jess started chuckling too. Soon the two girls were rolling about in the water, howling with laughter.

"Come on," said Cammie finally, wiping her eyes with her fin. "We'd better get to work...or else we'll need some sea dragon magic to help us finish our projects on time!"

Chapter Four

Over the next few days, Cammie worked hard
on her project. Soon her fins ached from gluing
all the tiny pebbles into place, but it looked
wonderful! She gazed down at her nearly-
finished mosaic, feeling proud.

Then it was time for their next Pearlies
meeting. As usual, Cammie and Jess swam

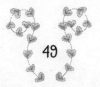

there together, talking non-stop. "My story's coming along really well," said Jess. "I've put in almost all the dangers that Miss Swish told us about. Now I just need to add a shark!" Her eyes gleamed.

Cammie hoped that Jessy wasn't about to get eaten! "My project's going well, too," she said. They glided around a group of clownfish. "I've done all the creatures who live in the Deep now, and—"

Suddenly Cammie paused. What was that, behind them? "Jess!" she hissed. "I think someone's following us."

Her best friend looked startled. "Really?" She glanced over her shoulder. "I think you're right!" she exclaimed. "I just saw someone duck behind that piece of purple coral."

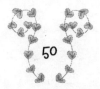

"I bet it's Fizz, playing a trick on us," whispered Cammie. "Come on, let's keep going. Maybe we can surprise her!"

The two seahorses swam on, talking as if they hadn't noticed anything. At first nothing happened. Then, peeking back, Cammie saw someone sneak out from behind the purple coral. She whirled around.

"Got you!" she cried. Then her mouth fell open. It was Tigg! "Oh, no!" she said, swimming over to her. "What are *you* doing here? You're supposed to be at home!"

To Cammie's annoyance, Tigg didn't even look guilty. "I know, but I want to come to Pearlies with you and Jess," she said. "Can I? Please, please?" She fluttered her fins, looking from one to the other.

Cammie shook her head crossly. "You know you can't! You're too young, it's not allowed."

"But I want to hear more about the sea dragon," protested Tigg. "Can't I just wait outside, and listen?"

"*No*," snapped Cammie. She grabbed Tigg's fin. "Come on, I've got to take you home now.

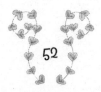

I'm going to be late for Pearlies because of you!"

Tigg jerked away. "I don't want to go home! I told you, I want to hear more about the sea dragon!"

"I'll come too," said Jess hastily. "And I'll tell you a story about the sea dragon on the way, but then you've *got* to stay at home after that. Promise?"

Tigg nodded so hard that she made currents in the water. "I promise," she said eagerly. "I want to hear a story about the wishes he grants! Will he grant just *any* wish? And how do you get him to grant one?"

Cammie looked sharply at her little sister as they started for home again. Did Tigg still think the sea dragon's magic was real? She opened her mouth to say something, but just then Jess began her story.

"Once upon a time, there was a crab with a terrible problem," said Jess.

"What?" gasped Tigg. A group of silvery fish darted past.

"His claws wouldn't click!" said Jess. "The poor crab felt like such a loser. All the other crabs laughed at him. So one day, the crab

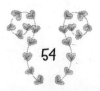

decided that he'd go and see the sea dragon, and wish for clicking claws..."

Jess went on with her story as they swam past the bright corals of Rainbow Reef. Tigg hung on her every word. By the time they reached home again, the crab had been granted a wish from the sea dragon, and had the clickiest claws of all.

"Wow!" breathed Tigg. "So all you have to do is *ask* the sea dragon, right? And if he feels sorry for you, then he'll help you, right?"

Jess held back a smile. "Well..."

"Tigg, you know that the sea dragon isn't *really* magical, don't you?" put in Cammie. "It's only a story!"

But Tigg was already swimming inside.

"Thanks, Jess. That was wavy!" she called over her shoulder.

Dad appeared in the doorway, wearing an apron and stirring something in a bowl. "What are you two doing here?" he said in surprise.

Cammie explained, and Dad groaned. "The little shrimp! I didn't even see her leave. Go on now — if you hurry, you won't miss too much."

Cammie and Jess swam back as fast as they could, zipping around rocks and pieces of coral. Even so, their Pearlie meeting had already begun by the time they reached the Pavilion.

"Sorry we're late, Miss Swish," panted Jess as they took their seats.

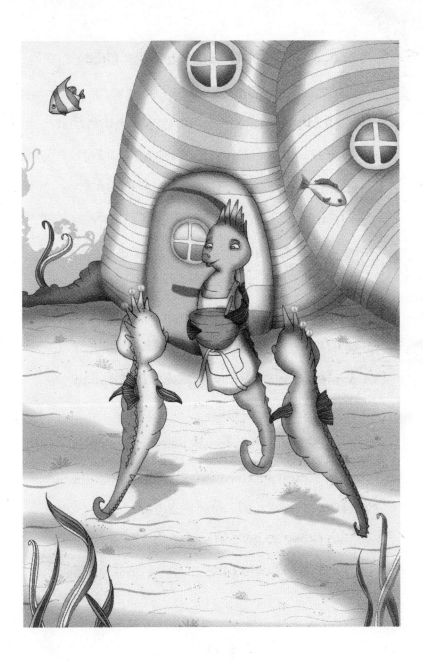

"That's all right," said Miss Swish kindly. "I was just explaining that we're going to try for our Sea Safety pearls next time. So I hope that everyone's projects are nearly ready.'

Cammie nodded with the others. Her eyes were shining. She could hardly wait for Miss Swish to see the beautiful mosaic she was making.

"And, if everyone wins their pearl, I'll have a special treat for you," went on Miss Swish. "A party, to celebrate being over halfway to becoming Seahorse Stars!"

A party! The girls looked eagerly at each other. Corinetta tossed her head. "Well, I'm sure I'll get *my* pearl," she bragged. "Just wait until you see my project!"

"Miss Swish, what if one of us doesn't get

her pearl?" asked Cora worriedly. "Will we still have a party?"

"We'll see," said Miss Swish with a smile. "I'm sure that you'll all do very well, though. Now, let's go over a few things, and then we'll go for a nature swim!"

Thinking of her mosaic, Cammie felt as certain as Corinetta that she'd get her pearl. Though in the past she'd been too confident and had done badly, she knew this wasn't the same at all. She'd worked really hard this time!

What could possibly go wrong?

Chapter Five

"Tigg, what are you doing?" asked Cammie

a few days later. She had just swum into their

bedroom. Tigg was holding her mosaic, staring

down at it.

Tigg's cheeks turned red. "Nothing," she

said. "I just wanted to see it, that's all."

Cammie swam quickly over. Her mosaic had

been tucked safely away under her bed. Tigg
had no business getting it out!

"Here, give it back," she ordered. "I have
to try for my pearl tomorrow, and I don't want
you to mess it up."

"I wasn't *messing it up*," protested Tigg. "I
was only looking!" She shoved the mosaic at
Cammie and swam off in a huff.

To Cammie's relief, she saw that Tigg hadn't damaged it. She smiled down at her finished mosaic. It was so bright and colourful, with the dangers of Rainbow Reef and the Deep all laid out in a map. Miss Swish was sure to be impressed!

Then Cammie frowned. Why had Tigg wanted to see it? She'd had such a serious expression on her face, too, as if...

Cammie shook her head. She was imagining things. Tigg was just being nosy — and that was certainly nothing new!

But that night at dinner, Cammie saw that Tigg had a secretive smile on her face. She didn't even seem upset when Stripe talked about how much fun he was having with Horace, his new friend.

"Me and Horace are building a coral camp
in his back garden!" he said. "It's a private den
that's just for us. And we're going to start a
club, too!"

Dad was handing out bowls of seaweed
soup. "Just the two of you?" he said. "That's
a rather small club. Why don't you ask Tigg
to join?"

Stripe played with his soup. "Well...Horace
says it's better to have just boys," he muttered.

Tigg tossed her head. "That's okay, Dad. I
don't want to join their stupid club." She
smirked at Stripe. "Anyway, I have a secret that
you don't know about!"

"What secret?" demanded Stripe hotly.

"Ha! Don't you wish you knew!" sang Tigg.
She giggled into her soup.

"That's enough, you two," said Mum with a sigh. Like the rest of the family, Cammie knew that she was tired of Stripe and Tigg not getting along. Life was much easier when the twins were friends!

Dad changed the subject. "Cammie, isn't tomorrow when you try for your pearl?" he asked.

Cammie nodded hard. "Yes, and I can hardly wait. I've learned *so* much about Sea Safety. I hope Miss Swish likes my mosaic."

"I'm sure she will," said Mum with a smile. "You've done a wonderful job!"

She and Dad started talking about grown-up things then, and Cammie gazed across the table at her little sister. Tigg was still smiling. In fact, she looked very pleased with herself!

But why? thought Cammie in confusion. What was her little sister up to?

Then she shook herself. It was probably just something silly. She had much more important things to worry about...like getting her pearl tomorrow!

Jess came by for Cammie the next day, so that the two girls could go to Pearlies together.

"Are you ready?" she asked with a grin when Cammie opened the door. She was holding the story she'd written. Cammie saw that she'd put it between two brightly coloured shells, just like a real book.

Cammie smiled back at her best friend.

"Yep! Let me just get my mosaic, and we can go!"

She swam into her bedroom with Jess following after her. "It's just under my bed," explained Cammie, ducking down in the water. "I wanted to keep it safe, so that—" She broke off, staring at the empty space under her bed.

"Jess! It's not here!" she gasped. She swept her fin all under her bed, just to be certain. But the mosaic was gone.

"Maybe you put it somewhere else and forgot," suggested Jess.

"No, I'm sure I didn't!" cried Cammie. But she searched anyway, pulling out drawers and even swimming up to look on her coral shelves. Her mosaic was nowhere to be seen!

"What's wrong?" asked Dad, appearing in the doorway.

"My mosaic is gone!" said Cammie. She felt
close to tears. She'd worked so hard on it!

"Gone?" repeated Dad in surprise. "But how
can it be? Here, I'll help you look. Jess, why

don't you go on to Pearlies? There's no point in both of you being late."

Part of Cammie wanted her friend to stay and help her look, but she knew that was selfish. She managed a smile. "Yes, go on, Jess," she said. "Tell Miss Swish I'll be there soon."

Jess looked worried. "Well...okay. I hope you find it, Cammie." She swam off, gazing back over her shoulder.

Cammie and Dad searched everywhere in the house that they could think of...but it was as if Cammie's mosaic had vanished into thin water. Suddenly Cammie thought of something.

"Where's Tigg?" she burst out. "She was looking at it yesterday! Maybe she took it!"

Dad shook his head. "She's out playing," he

said. "I saw her just a little while ago, and she didn't have it then."

"Oh," said Cammie, her fins drooping. She had been so sure!

Finally Dad looked at the coral clock and said, "Cammie, you're already late. Why don't you go on, and explain to Miss Swish what happened? I'm sure she'll let you try for your pearl next week, once we've found it."

"But I'll be the only Dancing Wave there without a project!" wailed Cammie.

"I know," said Dad, patting her fin. "But you need to go anyway, and explain to Miss Swish. I'll keep looking while you're gone."

Cammie knew he was right, but she still felt like crying! "All right," she mumbled. "I'll...I'll see you later, then."

Saying goodbye, she slowly swam off. This was awful – she'd have to tell everyone that she didn't have a project after all. Even worse, she'd probably be the only Dancing Wave not to get her pearl this week. They might not even have a party now, because of her!

As Cammie swam sadly along, she spotted something lying on the sandy sea floor. Her eyes widened.

It was a small, round blue pebble...just like the ones she'd used for her mosaic.

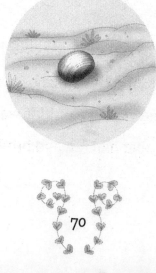

Chapter Six

That doesn't mean anything, thought Cammie as she stared at the pebble. *Those pebbles are everywhere!*

Then she spotted another one, lying a little distance away. And there was one of the shells she'd used. She was sure of it! It was an almost perfect circle, and had red and brown spots.

Beyond it were more pebbles, leading off over the sand.

Cammie's pink fins felt hot with anger. Someone had taken her mosaic, and had gone off somewhere with it. *Well, I'm going to get it back — right now!* thought Cammie. She shot off, following the trail of pebbles.

It wasn't easy. A gentle current stirred the warm waters of Rainbow Reef, so that many of the pebbles were half-covered by sand. Cammie had to concentrate hard, gazing down at the sandy floor. There was a pebble...and another one...and a shell...

After a while, Cammie looked up and blinked. She hadn't realized that she'd come so far. She was almost at the end of Rainbow Reef! Beyond lay the Deep.

Cammie shivered as she stared out at the dark, deep water. She'd never been so close to the Deep before. It looked just as scary as she'd imagined. Then she remembered her Sea Safety lessons, and frowned thoughtfully. Wasn't this near to where the sea dragon lived?

The sea dragon! Cammie gasped. Suddenly

she realized what had happened. It *had* been Tigg who'd taken her mosaic — to use as a map. And now she'd gone to see the sea dragon, to ask him to grant a wish!

Cammie darted to the edge of the Deep. "Tigg!" she shouted. "Tigg, where are you?"

There was no reply. *I've got to go and get Dad!* thought Cammie fearfully. But there was no time. If Tigg was in the Deep, then *anything* could happen to her. She might even get eaten by a shark!

Cammie gulped. Miss Swish had told them never to go into the Deep alone…but she knew she didn't have a choice. She had to find her sister!

Trembling, she dived into the Deep. The water grew cold around her. Cammie swam deeper and deeper, feeling smaller and smaller as she went. It was so dark down here! She peered around her, trying to see.

"Tigg!" she called again. "TIGG!"

All at once Cammie spotted something swimming ahead of her. She stopped short, staring. She'd never seen such a strange-looking creature! He looked like a seahorse, only he swam on his stomach, like a fish. And he was covered with long, fluttery fins, as if he was wearing a cape.

The sea dragon! realized Cammie suddenly. She raced up to him. She knew he liked to be left alone, but she had to talk to him!

"Excuse me," she said timidly. "I need to ask you—"

The sea dragon's eyes flashed. "Harrumph!"

he snorted. "Not *another* one!" He turned and swam away.

Cammie hurried after him. "Another one?" she cried, bobbing in front of him. "Oh, please tell me — have you seen my sister? She's smaller than me, and has black and orange stripes, and—"

"Stop chattering!" moaned the sea dragon, putting his fins over his ears. "Isn't one of you enough for one day? All I want is some peace and quiet!"

Cammie glared at him. Tigg might be down here in the Deep somewhere, and the sea dragon didn't even care!

"You have to tell me if you've seen her," she said. "Or else I'll *never* go away. I'll...I'll follow you around, talking, and singing, and—"

"No!" gasped the sea dragon, looking horrified. "All right, there was a very small seahorse here a while ago. Most irritating! She kept going on about magic, and wishes, and I don't know *what* rubbish..."

"Yes, that's her!" cried Cammie. Hope swept through her. "Where is she? What happened?"

The sea dragon shrugged. "I told her I didn't know what she was talking about, and to go away! She left in a hurry — that way, I think." He pointed. "Now, will you *please* leave me alone?" He swam off without waiting for an answer. His long, fluttery fins streamed behind him.

Cammie stared in the direction he'd pointed. Oh, poor Tigg! She'd come here thinking that the sea dragon could do magic, and then he wouldn't even talk to her. She must be so upset!

But where had she gone? The Deep was such a big place! Cammie started off, feeling even smaller and colder than before. "Tigg, where are you?" she shouted into the gloom. "Tigg! Please answer me!"

Suddenly Cammie stifled a shriek. There was something moving, down there in the darkness. It was a creature larger than any she'd ever seen, with a soft, floppy body and lots of arms.

A giant squid! thought Cammie in a panic.

Miss Swish had told them that giant squids would shoot black goo at you, and maybe even eat you! She started to swim off as fast as she could – but then she stopped, staring in horror.

Barely visible in the gloom, Cammie saw her little sister…frozen in panic, right in the giant squid's path!

Chapter Seven

Cammie raced towards her little sister. "Tigg!"
she screamed. "Tigg, hurry! We have to get
away!"

The giant squid was so huge that Cammie
could hardly see anything else. It moved
forward, waving its arms. Tigg stared at it,
trembling with fear. "Cammie!" she moaned,

holding the mosaic to her chest. "Oh, Cammie, make it go away!"

"Come on!" Cammie grabbed Tigg's fin and shot off. The squid roared in anger and followed. Cammie could feel it rushing towards them through the water, bigger than anything she'd ever imagined.

"*Hurry*," she panted to Tigg.

But she knew it was no use. Her little sister was swimming as hard as she could, but it just wasn't fast enough. The giant squid was getting closer and closer. Any second now it would shoot black goo at them, and then they'd be done for!

Suddenly Cammie had an idea. She remembered Mum saying that giant squids weren't very clever. Could she trick it, somehow?

Her heart thudding, Cammie spun about in the water. "You don't scare me, you big sand-brain!" she shouted at the squid. "I bet you don't even *have* any black goo!" She stuck her tongue out at it, and wiggled her tail.

Tigg gaped at her. "*Cammie!* What are you

doing?" She tugged at Cammie's fin, trying to pull her along.

Cammie wasn't sure, either! She just knew this was their only chance. She shouted again, "Go on, shoot your black goo at us! I bet you can't, you big phoney!"

"PHONEY?" thundered the squid. "Take this, you little shrimps!"

"Get ready," Cammie whispered to Tigg.

Whoosh! A cloud of black goo barrelled towards them.

"*Now!*" cried Cammie. Swimming as hard as she could, she pulled her little sister after her. Ducking away from the cloud, they jetted right over the giant squid's head. A moment later, the spot where they'd been was inky black.

Cammie kept swimming, faster than she'd ever swum before. They had to get back to Rainbow Reef, before...

"HEY!" bellowed the giant squid. "You're not there!"

Peering over her shoulder, Cammie saw the squid searching the cloud of goo. He looked up — and spotted her! "There you are," he snarled, coming after them. "You tricked me!"

"SWIM!" screamed Cammie to Tigg. She put on a burst of speed, zipping upwards.

"I am, I am!" sobbed Tigg, still clinging to the mosaic.

The squid spun his arms around, shooting through the water. Looking back again, Cammie screamed. He was so close now that all she could see was his eyes, glaring at her!

Rainbow Reef lay just ahead. Dragging Tigg behind her, Cammie burst into the familiar waters of home.

She smiled in relief…and then shrieked as she saw the squid was still following them! He'd been slowed down at first by the shallow water, but now he was gaining on them again.

"You don't get away *that* easy!" he boomed.

Tigg's tail was drooping. "I can't swim any more," she whimpered. "I'm too tired."

"Tigg, you *have* to," Cammie begged, pulling her sister along. The squid was just behind them! If only they could hide...but she didn't see a single cave anywhere.

"Ha, ha!" chortled the squid. "You two are going to be very tasty, I can tell!"

Suddenly Cammie's eyes widened. Wasn't the whirlpool near here? Yes, there was the *DANGER* sign! Perhaps, if she was quick...

"Tigg, you're going to have to swim just a little bit more," she whispered. "Head towards the whirlpool with me, as fast as you can! Then when I say GO, we'll swim off to the left."

Tigg nodded weakly. "I'll try!"

The two seahorses shot towards the whirlpool. Cammie gulped as she saw it. It was like a huge cyclone in the water, with sand and pieces of coral flying about in it.

The squid roared to see them getting away. "Oh, no you don't!" he shouted. He raced after them, his arms spinning.

Cammie got as near to the whirlpool as she dared. "GO!" she shouted. But she'd got too close. Before she knew what had happened, she and Tigg had been sucked right in!

"Eek!" screamed Cammie. She held tightly

to Tigg's fin. The water tumbled them head over tail, round and round. Tigg shrieked, clinging to the mosaic. Suddenly it was torn away from her, and went spinning off into the water. Cammie hardly noticed. She struggled wildly. They had to get free!

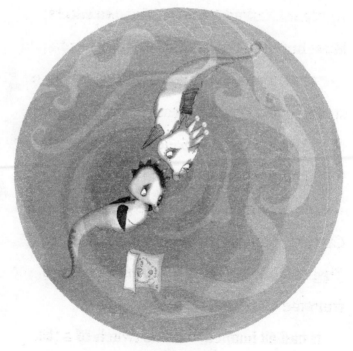

Then Cammie remembered what Miss Swish had told them. Struggling wouldn't help at all. She forced herself to stay calm. "Just relax, and swim when I tell you!" she shouted to Tigg. A moment later, the whirlpool had taken them back to its edge.

"Now!" called Cammie. The two sisters burst out of the current. They were free!

"Ohh," groaned Cammie dizzily, trying to stay upright. Her head was spinning just like the whirlpool. Tigg looked woozy too – she was practically swimming sideways! But there was no time to lose. Grabbing Tigg's fin, Cammie managed to drag them both away. Tigg quickly snatched up Cammie's mosaic from the sand as they passed it.

It had all happened in the twitch of a tail.

The squid was still coming after them, heading right for the whirlpool. "ARGH!" he bellowed as he got swept up in it.

From a safe distance, Cammie and Tigg watched with open mouths. The giant squid spun round and round, his arms flailing.

Cammie almost felt guilty, and then told herself not to be silly. The squid had been planning to eat them!

Finally the squid got free. "My head," he moaned, clutching it with his arms. "I'm never coming *here* again!" And he swam dizzily off, back towards the Deep.

"Cammie, you did it!" cried Tigg, bouncing up and down. "You're the best sister ever!"

Cammie hugged Tigg hard. She knew she should be angry with her for all the trouble she'd caused, but somehow she wasn't. She was just glad her little sister was all right!

Then she sighed. What were their parents going to think, when they found out about this? She and Tigg would be in terrible trouble. Cammie decided not to think about that, just yet.

"Come on," she said, linking her tail through Tigg's. "Let's go home!"

Chapter Eight

Cammie and Tigg started off. They had hardly

swum any distance at all when a voice called,

"There you are!"

"Dad!" cried Cammie as their father came

racing up. Just behind him was Miss Swish.

"Oh, thank Neptune you're all right!" said

Miss Swish. "I got worried when you didn't

arrive, after Jess said you were on your way."

Dad hugged Cammie and Tigg tightly.
"Yes, Miss Swish came and told me, and then
I realized Tigg was missing as well! What
happened?"

Cammie hesitated. Dad was going to be
furious when he found out that they'd gone
into the Deep! And what would Miss Swish

say? She'd think that Cammie hadn't listened to her about all the dangers there.

She bit her lip. "Well…"

Suddenly Tigg piped up. "It's…it's all my fault, Dad," she said. "I wanted to go and see the sea dragon."

"The sea dragon!" repeated Dad in horror.

"But he lives in the Deep!" exclaimed Miss Swish.

Tigg nodded, hanging her head. "Jess told me he was magical, and could grant wishes."

"She was only teasing," said Cammie quickly. "We told Tigg it wasn't really true, but—"

"I didn't believe you," mumbled Tigg. "I thought you were just saying that so I wouldn't try to go and see him. I…I took Cammie's mosaic, so that I could find the way." She held it up.

Cammie stared at it sadly. Her beautiful mosaic was ruined! Almost all the pebbles and shells had fallen off. You could hardly even tell what the pictures were now.

"I'm sorry, Cammie," whispered Tigg. "I didn't mean to spoil it."

Cammie managed a smile. "I know," she said. "It's okay." It wasn't, of course! But Tigg looked so miserable that she couldn't say anything else. And the most important thing was that they were both safe.

Miss Swish put a comforting fin on Cammie's shoulder. "I can tell you put a lot of work into your project," she said. "I'm sorry it got ruined."

"Now, I want to know exactly what happened," said Dad sternly. "Tigg, I thought you were playing outside! You know you're not to go beyond the pink coral."

With both sisters explaining, the story came out: how Tigg had sneaked back into the house to get Cammie's mosaic, and how Cammie had followed the trail of pebbles to the Deep.

Cammie took a deep breath. "And...well, I know I'm not supposed to go into the Deep on my own. But I was afraid if I came back for help, something might happen to Tigg." She told them how she'd swum into the Deep, and met the sea dragon.

"I was right, he *is* stuck-up," muttered Tigg, scuffing the sand with her tail. "He's horrible!"

"He showed me which way Tigg had gone, and I went after her," continued Cammie. "And then..." She explained about the squid, and how they'd got away from him.

Dad and Miss Swish were staring at her with their mouths open.

"Cammie!" cried Dad. "That was *very* dangerous." Then he hugged her tightly. "But

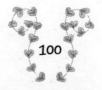

it was very brave, too," he added. "You saved Tigg's life!"

Miss Swish nodded proudly. "Well done, Cammie! I couldn't have done better myself."

Cammie ducked her head shyly, feeling warm inside from the praise. She'd been so afraid that everyone would be angry!

"But you are NEVER to go into the Deep on your own again," said Dad. "Either of you! Is that understood?"

"Yes, Dad," said Cammie and Tigg together. Cammie shivered. Dad didn't have to worry. She never wanted to go back there again!

"And Tigg, I'm afraid you're going to have to be punished," said Dad. "I can't have you sneaking off like that. Not to mention taking Cammie's mosaic without permission!

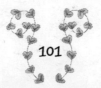

Does being grounded for a week sound fair to you?"

Tigg nodded sadly, staring down at the sand. Cammie felt sorry for her little sister, but she thought Dad was being very fair.

He hugged Tigg close. "All right, then. Let's go home. Cammie, would you like to go back to Pearlies with Miss Swish? I think the party is still going on."

"Party?" Cammie blinked in confusion. "But...not everyone got their pearl."

"Everyone who was there did," smiled Miss Swish. "And as soon as we get back, you'll get yours, too."

"*Really?*" gasped Cammie, bouncing in the water.

"Yes, really," laughed Miss Swish. "You've earned it, Cammie. Your sea safety skills are clearly top-notch!"

Cammie was so thrilled she couldn't speak. She had got her pearl after all!

"Go on," said Dad with a smile. He nudged her with his fin. "Have fun at the party, Cammie. You deserve it!"

* * *

That night at dinner, Cammie thought she'd never been happier. On her crown was a fourth shiny pearl. And the party that afternoon had been amazing! All of the other Dancing Waves had earned their pearls, too. They'd been agog to hear about her journey to the Deep…even Corinetta.

Cammie grinned as she remembered Corinetta's project. The golden seahorse had done a drawing showing herself using sea safety skills. The Corinetta in the drawing had looked every bit as snooty as in real life!

And Jess had read her story aloud again, so that Cammie could hear it. They'd all shrieked with laughter at the hapless Jessy's adventures. Yes, it had been a brilliant party, thought Cammie contentedly.

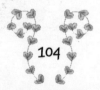

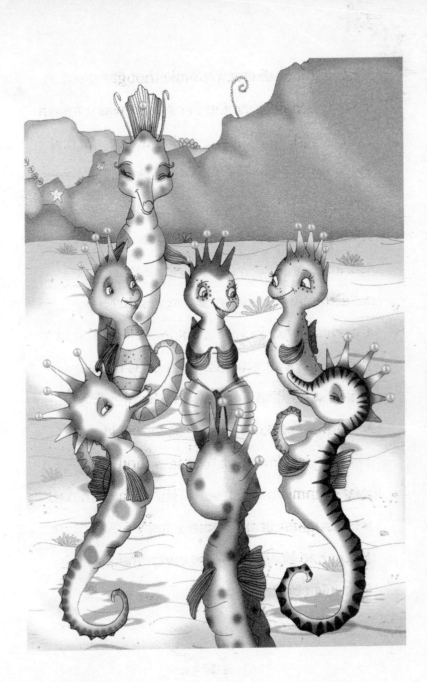

She held back a yawn. Now that the day was almost over with, she was very tired!

Mum smiled at her. "It's hard work fighting squids, isn't it?" she teased.

Cammie smiled back. She knew Mum was proud of her, too. What a fantastic day this had turned out to be! And it had started out so terribly.

Stripe looked grumpy. He'd been playing with Horace all afternoon, and had been very cross to realize he'd missed all the excitement. "There's just one thing," he said suddenly, looking up from his stew. "Tigg, what wish did you want the sea dragon to grant?"

Cammie glanced at Tigg curiously. She'd never even thought to ask that!

Tigg's cheeks were flushed. "It was stupid," she muttered.

"You don't have to tell us if you don't want to," said Dad.

Tigg shrugged. "Well...I was going to ask him to make me and Stripe friends again."

Cammie felt a pang. Oh, poor Tigg! She had been so unhappy without her twin brother to play with.

Stripe opened his mouth, and then closed it again. "Really?" he said finally.

"Yes," said Tigg. "I told you it was stupid!"

"I think Tigg's missed you a lot, Stripe," put in Mum gently. "It's been very hard on her, being on her own so much lately."

Stripe stared down at the coral table. He cleared his throat. "Tigg, I...um, I mean...

would you like to play with me and Horace sometime?"

Tigg looked up cautiously. "I thought Horace wouldn't play with a *girl*."

"Well, I don't care!" burst out Stripe. "His ideas aren't nearly as good as yours. If he won't let you play with us, then...then you and I can make our *own* camp!"

"Yeah!" cried Tigg. Her face lit up. "I've got lots of ideas for one!"

"Good, I'm glad that's settled," said Dad with a smile. "Now come on, you two. Time to get ready for bed!"

As the twins raced off, still chatting eagerly, Cammie realized that her day had just got better. Not only did she have her fourth pearl, but her brother and sister were friends again.

Cammie smiled upwards, admiring her four pearls. She could hardly believe it, but she was over halfway to becoming a Seahorse Star. Soon it would be time to try for her fifth pearl...and she could hardly wait!

The End

Dive in with Cammie and her friends and
collect every splash-tastic tale in

Seahorse Stars!

The First Pearl ISBN 9781409520245

Cammie is thrilled to be a member of the Pearlies
— the waviest club in Rainbow Reef. Her first task
is to go camping. Will she keep her cool, or
is she in too deep?

First-Aid Friends ISBN 9781409520252

When Cammie's best friend shows a natural talent for
first-aid, Cammie gets competitive...and soon it's their
friendship that needs patching up!

The Lost Lagoon ISBN 9781409520269

Cammie is confused by compasses and lost when
it comes to maps, so earning her Wave Wanderer
pearl is proving tricky. When stuck-up Corinetta
offers to help, Cammie is grateful. But can
Corinetta be trusted?

Danger in the Deep ISBN 9781409520276

Cammie loves studying for her Sea Safety pearl
and learning about the dangers of the Deep. So when
her little sister disappears, it's up to Cammie
to rescue her...

Coming soon...

Dancing Waves ISBN 9781409520306

All the seahorses must work together if they are
to earn their Tidal Team pearl...and they've chosen
Cammie as their team leader. Can she stop them
squabbling and help them come out on top?

The Rainbow Queen ISBN 9781409520313

To get her last Proficiency Pearl, Cammie must do
a good deed in Rainbow Reef...and then she will be a
Seahorse Star! But when Cammie begins her task, she
realizes the Reef is in danger, and she must ask
the Queen for help.

For more wonderfully wavy reads
check out
www.fiction.usborne.com